For God loves a cheerful giver.

—2 Corinthians 9:7

ZONDERKIDZ

The Berenstain Bears Learn to Share
Previously published by Reader's Digest Kids in 1992 as *The Berenstain Bears Learn to Share*
Copyright © 1992, 2010 by Berenstains, Inc.
Illustrations © 1992, 2010 by Berenstains, Inc.

Requests for information should be addressed to:

Zonderkidz, *Grand Rapids, Michigan 49530*

Library of Congress Cataloging-in-Publication Data

Berenstain, Stan, 1923–2005
    The Berenstain Bears learn to share / created by Stan and Jan Berenstain ; with
Mike Berenstain.
        p.   cm.
    Summary: With the help of Jesus, Sister Bear learns to share her toys and to play with
other bears.
    ISBN 978-0-310-71939-7 (hardcover)
    [1. Stories in rhyme. 2. Sharing—Fiction 3. Christian life—Fiction. 5. Bears—Fiction.]
I. Berenstain, Jan, 1923- II. Berenstain, Michael. III. Title.
    PZ8.3.B4493Bhdw 2010
    [E]—dc22   2009037060

Editor: Mary Hassinger
Art direction: Cindy Davis

Printed in China

10 11 12 13 14 15 /LPC/ 28 27 26 25 24 23 22 21 20 19 18 17 16 15 14 13 12 11 10 9 8 7 6 5 4

The Berenstain Bears

Learn to Share

by Stan and Jan Berenstain
with Mike Berenstain

ZONDERVAN.com/
AUTHORTRACKER
follow your favorite authors

ZONDERkidz

Living Lights™

I'm Sister Bear.
I'm here to say
that what I like
to do is PLAY.

I run.

I skip.

I jump.

I climb.

I have myself
a great old time!

Who's the one
I play with best,
pray and sing with
more than the rest?

Just turn the page
and you will see
my favorite playmate—

little me!

It's lots of fun
to play you see.
I ask my dolls
to come to tea.

I have my games
all to myself,
and every toy
on each big shelf.

But Mama says
almost every day,
"Take time to share.
Take time to pray."

But there are times
I do not care.
My things are mine!
They aren't to share!

I take each turn
on my red truck.

I do not share
my pull-toy duck.

I say inside,
"It's all mine!"
But then I wonder,
is that kind?

Is this the way
that I should be?
A bear that only
thinks of me?

Then I know
it's time to share
my playthings with
my fellow bear.

One is fun,
but it is true
that many games
are best with two.

When I am sure
I need another,
I go look
for my big brother.

We play checkers,

beanbags,

pick-up-sticks.

Spending time with Brother
I get my kicks.

Look! Here come Liz
and Bob and Clem.
Now we can share
with *all* of them.

I ride Bob's bike.
He rides my trike.
It's great. We share
and share alike.

So, sharing's fun.
It's good to do,
and lots of times—
it's easy, too.

And if you share
it's also true
your fellow bear
will share with you!

We share our time
when we're together.
We run, we hide,
skip stones—whatever.

We share our books.

We trade our cards.

We visit one
another's yards.

Now we are more
than three or four.
We're five, six, seven,
and lots, lots more!

Here come Millie,
Mike, and Nat.
Anna May has brought
her cat.

Here comes Fred
with Snuff, his terrier!
This way, friends!
The more the merrier!

Remember Jesus says
that he is with you
when more are together—
like five, four, three,
or two.

This way, cubs!
Come one! Come all!
We'll choose up sides
to play baseball.

A game of ball
is lots of fun.
We pitch. We bat.
Look! Too-Tall hit
a big home run!

It works out well
if you can share
your playthings
with your fellow bear.

The ball is mine.
It's Freddy's bat.
Lizzy brought
a glove and hat.

She'll share her hat
but not her glove.
Uh-oh! Fred gives her
a little shove.

We all saw
that little shove!
It was not showing
God's care and love.

Soon, there are lots
of arguments.

Of course, I put in
my two cents.

This is not the way.
It's not right!
We should all be sharing,
not in a fight.

And so to keep
the peace between us,
all our friends go home.

"Please think of Jesus.
He would want us to share
and show we love
our fellow bear."

Meanwhile, friends,
it's still today.
And there is still
some time to play.
So turn the page,
and you will see...

Brother, will you
play with me?